CURIOUS RABBINIC TALES

The Shortest Tall Stories

PROFESSOR MIRIAM HOFFMAN

Yi Jewish
A Division of Yiddishkayt Initiative

A Division of Yiddishkayt Initiative

Coral Springs, Florida
www.YILoveJewish.org

Copyright © 2020 Miriam Hoffman

Print ISBN: 978-0-9993365-5-7

Edited by Carol Killman Rosenberg
www.carolkillmanrosenberg.com

Cover and interior by Gary A. Rosenberg
www.garyarosenberg.com

Printed in the United States of America

Contents

CURIOUS RABBINIC TALES

Introduction

Folktales belong to the earliest folk literature, likely predating Jewish sources. Once they were adapted into the Jewish setting, they were integrated into our own mythology. Folktales were told as parables with a moral undercurrent to expose human frailty and strength, vanity and heroism.

The Jewish folktale encompasses wit and wisdom, evil and goodness, breaking down established norms, unmasking foolish pride, and fighting against injustice. The following tales and legends tell of miracles, heroism, cowardice and above all, the poor folk and the wealthy ones. In short, anything we wouldn't say openly, we disguise as a parable or a folktale. These tales are our most treasured legacy.

IF YOU WANT PEOPLE TO THINK YOU ARE WISE, AGREE WITH THEM.

—YIDDISH PROVERB

The Maiden of Ludmir

The First and Only Female Hassidic Rabbi in the Ukraine

hanah Rukhele Verbermakher (1805–1888) was the name of the one and only Hassidic woman rabbi. She was called *"Tsadeykes* (virtuous woman). The true story begins with the "Tchernobiler preacher," Reb Motele, who had a great influence on his generation. His wish was considered an order, and even Misnagdim (opponents of the Hasidim) had great respect for him.

The Tchernobiler holy rebbe also had great influence on the Maiden of Ludmir, whose story was rare and note-worthy. It is a story that occurred at that remarkable time when the Hassidic movement was flourishing, when Jewish hearts were enchanted with the wonder-filled stories of the Hassidic rabbis and when Jewish imagination was in full bloom.

Ludmir, or Ludomir, was a little town in the Ukraine situated among other little Jewish towns where Jews were poverty stricken and consumed with eking out a living, but one thing was always paramount, and that was *"Avoy-das Haboyre"*—worship of the One Above.

Among the Jewish population, one could find great Torah scholars and pious Jews. And so in Ludmir lived a Jew named Monish Verbermakher, a good-hearted and pious man who constantly studied the Torah. His wife was barren, and after ten years of a childless marriage, the man had the right to divorce his wife.

So his wife approached her husband saying, "You know what, Monish? Maybe we should pay a visit to the Tchernobiler rabbi. He is known as a miracle worker. Maybe we should ask for his blessing."

"I'm not going!" said her husband, Monish. "It's your fault that we have no children, so you go by yourself and ask for your blessing."

"If that's the case," said his wife, "I will go by myself to ask for a blessing from the Tchernobiler Rebbe."

The rebbe welcomed her, wanting to know why she came, to which she replied, "Holy Rebbe! My husband and I have no children after ten years of marriage, so I came for your blessing."

The Rebbe soothed her saying, "I can understand how much you are suffering, and I have great compassion for you. All I can tell you is that the fault is not with you but with your husband. Therefore, I will bless you. Go back home with my blessing, but instead of a boy, you will have a girl to teach your husband a lesson."

So the woman returned home full of joy and shared the good news with her husband, and before the year was done, both became parents of a girl, Khanah Rukhele.

Khanah Rukhele grew up to be a brilliant girl and studied the Torah and the Talmud with her father.

"What a pity that Khanah Rukhele happens to be a girl," her father lamented, "instead of a boy. Had she been a boy, she would be considered a brilliant Torah scholar."

But her mother didn't let it go with that. "So what if she is a girl? She can still be everything a brilliant boy is capable of being. In fact, she will exceed boys in her brilliance."

And the mother taught her daughter to recite passages from the Torah, blessings, and prayers. Whenever her father would study the Torah and say the blessings, his daughter, Khanah Rukhele, would sit next to him and devour every word of his recitation of the Torah.

The father realized that his daughter was absorbing, with great appetite, every word he recited from the Holy Scriptures. He taught her passages from the Torah until she became a Torah scholar and then began concentrating on Talmudic works. She developed a deep appreciation for the Medresh and Aggadah, (the legends, the nonlegal texts in the Talmud), as well as the Mussar writings, the sacred books derived from the ethical writings of the rabbis.

The girl carried within her inner self a great soul and gained a great appreciation of all around her. The Jews of Ludmir called her "The wonderful Khanah Rukhele," appreciating that she was a righteous woman and one in a generation. Her name became known all over the Jewish communities in the Ukraine, and she became a legend. As time went by, she began to steep herself in the Gemarah, the Meforshim (the Torah commentators) as well as the Mussar, and this became her life's mission.

By the time Khanah Rukhele reached twelve or thirteen years of age, her fame had spread to all parts of Jewish Ukraine and the matchmakers began to break down her door with marriage proposals. A slew of Torah scholars, also wealthy men, flocked to ask for her hand. No dowry was requested; she was desired as she was.

Her father had the right to agree without a contractual handshake (meaning his daughter's consent), but he didn't approve of doing so as he had great respect for his daughter, but he shared the enticing proposals with his wife, Khanah Rukhele's mother.

"Monish!" she would say. "Why are you in such a hurry to marry her off? She is our only child! I don't anticipate her to be an old maid."

But her father insisted, "A girl must marry. Why wait?"

But the mother stood her ground. "A boy must also marry, so what? Our daughter harbors a great soul! We have to be careful. If she marries, she will leave us, and I don't approve yet. She is different from all other girls. She is busy concentrating on the Torah and other sacred books. Don't tear her away from them by making an ordinary woman out of her, who cooks and washes laundry and bears children."

"And that's the best reason to marry her off," replied Monish.

"You have no understanding of what I'm saying," replied her mother. "Our daughter possesses a sacred soul, a heavenly soul. She has the heart of a woman, the soul of a woman, but the time has not come yet to make a woman out of her."

A short time later, Khanah Rukhele's mother fell severely sick. An hour before the departure of her soul, she called her husband over and whispered, "I beg you, Monish, do nothing without our daughter's knowledge! Do not rush to marry her off."

To this, the father replied, "But whoever heard of parents asking their children for their opinion? It's the parents who decide the future of their children."

"But not when it comes to our daughter!" cried out her mother from her deathbed. "You must promise me that you will do nothing without her consent."

Monish, having no choice, promised. Soon after, Khanah Rukhele's mother passed away. The father and daughter said kaddish (the prayer for the dead) and mourned the mother's death. The death of Khanah Rukhele's mother made a great impression on her; she became even more pious.

Her father thought, *Once she is married, she will forget the great misfortune that befell us.* But then he remembered that he gave a solemn oath to his wife not to do anything without his daughter's will. Slowly he broached the subject with Khanah Rukhele, saying, "You know what, my child? Maybe it's time to think about finding you a match."

Khanah Rukhele lowered her eyes, her face reddened, and said nothing.

"Don't be embarrassed, my child," continued her father. "Marriage is also a Jewish tradition."

Khanah Rukhele replied, "You know, Father, I've already thought about it . . ."

Her father was elated. "I will call a matchmaker!"

"Please don't call matchmakers, Father. I have already chosen my future husband!"

"What are you saying, daughter?!" exclaimed her father. "*You* chose your future husband on your own?"

"Yes, Father, and I will marry him!"

"But who is he? A great Torah scholar?"

"I chose Dovidl, the son of Fayvish. Our neighbor's son."

Monish was incredulous. "What in the world made you think of him? He is a simple young man, no scholar! He has no stature, no money—"

"But I love him, Father!" she exclaimed.

"How does a Jewish girl come to such a thing as love?"

"My love for Dovidl is as strong as death and as sacred as divine fire!"

Monish suddenly realized that his daughter was serious, and this was not a joke. All he wanted to know was, "Why did you choose, Dovidl, of all people?"

So Khanah Rukhele opened up her heart and said, "I have been thinking of Dovidl for quite a while. I have no idea why. But one morning, I took a short walk before prayer, curious to see God's wonders—the heavens, the earth, and his entire creation.

"I was enchanted with every little flower, blade of grass, each tree, the birds singing God's praises—what a marvelous world the One Above had created—and suddenly before me stood a young man, eyes radiating joy, a face aflame with life, and that was Dovidl. Suddenly all my thoughts were mixed up. Everything looked like

Dovidl—his eyes reflected the heavens, his face reflected God's creation, the world—and when I heard his voice, I heard a choir of angels.

"He said, 'Khanah Rukhele, I heard so much about you! I always wanted to approach but didn't dare. How I wanted to speak to you, but you are known as the wonderful Khanah Rukhele.' And that was all he said, but his image remained with me. I hear his voice all around me, I see his image wherever I go, and if you are talking to me, Father, about a match, it must only be with Dovidl."

Monish was forced to send a matchmaker to Dovidl's father, Fayvish. All of the town of Ludmir buzzed with the news that Monish had sent a matchmaker to Fayvish to propose a match between his daughter and Fayvish's son, Dovidl. No one understood why Khanah Rukhele, who could pick and choose the best of matches, had chosen her neighbor's son, who seemed to have no special qualities for such an honor. The townspeople wondered if Dovidl possessed special merits unknown to them, if maybe he was one of the thirty-six righteous men who uphold the moral and ethical qualities of the world.

Khanah Rukhele herself was puzzled by the fact that she had fallen in love with Dovidl, having seen him only once, and she began to wonder whether he deserved her love. So she approached her father with this request, "Father! Before we write the *tnoyim* (conditions) of our marriage contract, I would like to speak with Dovidl face to face."

This frightened her father, who said to her, "Whoever heard of a Jewish girl falling in love with a boy and then wanting to speak with her future husband face to face before they are engaged? After you get married, you can speak to each other all the time."

The engagement ritual was written, and Dovidl was in seventh heaven with joy, but, according to tradition, the two young people were not allowed to converse yet. So Khanah Rukhele cried and prayed and set out on her own to visit her mother's grave in the cemetery. Her father warned her, "A bride is not allowed to go to the Holy Place alone!" But Khanah Rukhele disregarded his warnings; she was seen very often crying at her mother's graveside.

Her vigil went on for some time, until one night she fell asleep at her mother's graveside. When she woke up, it was already dark, and she became frightened and began to run among the gravestones. In her terror, she fell on one of the gravesites and, feeling as if somebody was pulling her down into the grave, she shouted for help and fainted.

Before dawn, Yosi, the gravedigger, heard somebody crying out. Knowing the dead don't speak, he thought to himself, *It must be a living person.* He took his lantern and went searching among the graves, thinking to himself, *Could it be Khayimkeh, the town madman?* Khayimkeh loved to visit the cemetery to laugh and cry, but this time Yosi had heard the voice of a girl.

Suddenly he found Khanah Rukhele in a faint. He lifted her up and brought her into the mortuary. The girl opened her eyes and understood nothing. The gravedigger carried her home, but she didn't even recognize her father.

The *shtetl* was in an uproar. A doctor was called while the girl lay silent on her bed, eyes closed. The doctor pronounced, "The girl is going to die!"

Her father was at his wits' end. *Right before her wedding,* he thought miserably, *and she is going to die?* He recited prayers with a quorum of men, but to no avail. Suddenly, Monish remembered the Tchernobiler rebbe and quickly set out for Tchernobil.

He approached the rebbe and pleaded, "Rebbe! You were the one who gave me this child—see to it that she stays alive!"

"Go back home!" said the rebbe. "Your daughter will get well, and you will have great joy raising her."

Her father was grateful and went home in peace. As soon as he got home, Khanah Rukhele opened her eyes, smiled at her father, and greeted him. Her father wept with joy. "Don't cry, Father," she said, "just sit next to my bed and listen to what I have to say."

Her father obeyed her, and he sat next to his daughter while she spun her tale.

"I want you to know that I am not the same Khanah Rukhele," she began. "I've changed, and now you must hear me out. When I woke up in the cemetery, I got frightened and began to run, but I fainted over a great Rebbe's grave. My soul left me and ascended to heaven, and I found myself standing in front of a celestial court as they were judging my soul. The judges didn't know what to do with me; they couldn't make up their minds whether I should live or die. A celestial defender was appointed to defend me, and he said I was a pious Jewish girl and deserved to live, that I was pure in my thoughts and performed good deeds.

"Then came the prosecutor who said awful things about me. He said I am not a woman like all other women—that all my good deeds are not natural and that I do things that are assigned only to men, that to study the Torah is assigned only for men. He said that within me there is a battle going on between a man and a woman and that I took on a man's station in life and refused to follow men's wishes and deeds.

"My defender insisted that I return to earth, get married, and be a wife to a man and a mother to our children. The prosecutor insisted that I must die and that there is no place for me on earth—that I will be no good for God or men. I felt that both sides were right, but that I wanted equal rights with men.

"The celestial court was at a loss, and they came to the Tchernobiler rebbe in his dreams wanting to know what to do with me. He set them straight, saying, 'In my merit Khanah Rukhele was born, but she chose her own path in life. She is blessed with her own mind and will. The best thing to do is to ask her directly what is to be done with her.'

"And so, Father, they approached me, wanting to know what should be done with me. So I didn't waste any time, and quoted from a passage in the Book of Psalms, *'Lo amut ki ekhye ve'esaper maasey adonoy!* I shall not die but live to tell the wondrous deeds of God.' I also quoted another passage, *'Lo hameytim hallelu adonoy.* The dead do not praise God.' I said to them, 'I want to live and continue to tell God's wonders, study God's Torah, and delve deeper into his secrets, but I've been punished with the fact that within me breathes a soul of a woman, and therefore, I am prevented from ascending higher and higher, so I demand to be given a new soul, a soul that can reach higher and higher.'

"The celestial quorum of judges still didn't know what to do with me, but when I awoke, I knew that I was given a noble soul, but I am not the same any longer." Khanah Rukhele's father had no idea what his daughter was talking about—that she had prevailed, had been given a new soul and had become a new Khanah Rukhele, not the same any longer. He didn't know whether to rejoice or fall into despair, but then he remembered the words of the Tchernobiler rebbe: "Remember, you will have great joy from your daughter, and also great pain."

As soon as Khanah Rukhele regained her strength, she got out of bed, stopped behaving like a woman and took on the obligations of a man. She dressed in *arbah kanfes, or tallis kotn,* (an undergarment worn by Orthodox Jews that covers the chest and the upper part of the back, tasseled on its four corners.) She donned a prayer shawl and began *leygn tefilin,* (binding a pair of black leather boxes to the left arm and the forehead during weekday morning prayers as required of observant male adults.)

Her father cried bitter tears. "But, Daughter, a woman is not obliged to follow all the commandments!"

But Khanah Rukhele earnestly took to the study of the Torah, the prayers, and the Talmud late into the night. Her father was frightened, thinking, *God forbid she has lost her mind altogether,* so he approached her. "But, Daughter, how will you accomplish all this when you are married?"

"Married!?" she cried out. She had entirely forgotten her engagement to Dovidl. "Oh yes, Father! I will have to send back the marriage contract to Dovidl!"

"To send back the marriage contract?!" shouted her father. "What will people say? If the match is not to your liking, we can find another one—"

"Father," she insisted, "you don't understand! I have decided *never* to get married. I don't want to be a woman any longer. I refuse to do a woman's chores. I want to be above all this! I want to dedicate my life to God."

She said it with such passion and conviction that her father was stumped. That same day, Khanah Rukhele sent the engagement proposition back to Dovidl, along with a little note she had written:

My dear Dovidl,

    I am sending back to you our engagement contract not because I don't love you any longer or because, God forbid, you have a defect. On the contrary, I am doing it because I was given a new soul in Heaven, and because I refuse to be like all other women. I found a new way in life, and I want to dedicate my entire life to the Torah, and because I was given a new soul, I want to keep my soul holy.
Forgive me,
Khanah Rukhele

Her father was brokenhearted. He didn't know whether his daughter was normal or about to lose her sanity, and even though she insisted that all this had come from above, he still insisted that she be like all the other girls, get married and bear children—but to no avail.

So Monish decided to pay another visit to the Tchernobiler rebbe, who said to him, "I understand your pain and your troubles. Your daughter is a lost soul, a glorious soul, searching for her own way in life. She found the path and wants to follow it. You must leave her alone."

Monish realized he had lost the battle, so he returned home never to bother his daughter again. Soon after, he began ailing and passed away. Khanah Rukhele said kaddish after him and sat *shiva* (the seven-day period of mourning.) After her father's death, she closed herself in her own world, secluded in a separate room dressed in a prayer shawl, praying and studying the Torah, chanting in her sweet voice the holy lines.

In the meantime, Khanah Rukhele's name began to be known throughout the Jewish communities in the Ukraine. With the money her father had left her, she built her own study house, and there she sat in her prayer shawl, separated from everybody. Jews came to pray and study the Torah in her synagogue, and she would pray along with them, but isolated in her own room. Men and women came to her synagogue asking for blessings, which she would give from behind her door.

A great number of Hassidim began believing in her, and hundreds gathered to listen to her interpreting the Torah. Many came with notes, like the ones placed into the cracks of the Wailing Wall in Jerusalem. Her reputation spread, and people who were sick and diseased went to her to be healed. Her followers were called "Hassidim of the Maiden of Ludmir."

But even as the fame and following of the Maiden of Ludmir grew, there was talk that she was possessed by a dybbuk. Many Hassidic rabbis refused to believe in her greatness. To think that a female "rebbe" should become so famous was outrageous to them, and they said that behind her door, where she sat solving problems, sat the devil, an evil spirit poking fun at the Torah and inclined to do harm to the Jews, and that it had possessed her. The people around her began to quarrel and break out in fistfights. Some wished to excommunicate her, others wanted to extract the dybbuk from within her, and still others insisted that she shed her manly traits and revert to being a woman.

Then, one Sabbath evening, her door opened, and she delivered an erudite discourse to her Hassidim. Prominent members of the community kept trying to persuade her to marry, and finally, at the age of forty, she married a Torah scholar whom the Tchernobiler rebbe recommended.

Her popularity waned after her marriage, and she later emigrated to the Holy Land, where she continued her mystical studies and engaged in rituals designed to hasten the coming of the Messiah.

More details can be found in the Encyclopaedia Judaica *and the tale told by the Tchernobiler Magid in D. L. Mekler's "Foon Rebn's Hoyf" p. 209.*

Az dos harts iz ful,
geyen di oygn iber.

When the heart is full,
the eyes overflow.

The One and Only Female Pope in the Vatican

Two great rebbes—Reb Motele Tchernobiler, of the Tchernobiler dynasty in the city of Tchernobil in the Ukraine, and Reb Yisroeltche Rizhiner, stemming from the city of Rizhin—conducted an exchange of dialogues and ideas. Each one of them had in mind to outdo the other in storytelling, and so Reb Yisroeltche Rizhiner began spinning his tale.

One day, a very distressed *khosid* (pious Jew) came rushing into the rebbe's house with a plea: "Rebbe! Only your blessing can save my wife from her difficult labor."

The rebbe, realizing that the man was distraught, comforted him. "Not only will I bless you, but I will tell you a story." And the Rizhiner began to spin his tale according to the Hassidic tradition:

This is a true story about a very bright young woman who lived in Rome, steeped in Catholic lore. But she couldn't attend the Catholic seminary due to the fact that she was a woman.

So she decided to disguise herself as a young man and attended the Catholic Academy of Rome. As an excellent and valued student of religion, she made a name for herself and, in time, was promoted to priesthood, then became a bishop, and then was appointed a cardinal. Of course, no one suspected that she was a woman, and the secret remained with her.

As time passed, the pope died, and the Vatican was about to select a new pope in Rome. A search began until they came upon this extraordinary cardinal, not suspecting that she was a woman, and proclaimed her pope over all Catholics.

As is well known, priests were sometimes inclined to transgress—to sin on the side—and so it was with the new pope, who whiled away nights in the streets and alleys of Rome where no one suspected that she was the pope. In the midst of this orgy, the female pope discovered that she was with child, and due to the fact that the pope wore wide garments, no one knew she was in the family way.

It all came to a head during the Christian holiday of Easter, when Rome was inundated with an enormous crowd of pilgrims who came from all over the world to partake in the Easter holiday. It is said that every year, at the same time, a great big podium was erected on the balcony of the Vatican, and this was the place where popes would deliver their papal sermons.

And the pope appeared, facing the big crowd, but in the midst of her sermon, she felt her labor pains coming on and before you knew it, she gave birth to a baby boy. The entire Vatican was thunderstruck, and the crowd outside was bewildered. How is it possible? How is it that the pope was a mother?

"But," concluded the Rizhiner rebbe, "it is known that everything is possible when it comes to the nations of the world, and the same goes for their holy scriptures."

Suddenly, the man who had come to the rebbe with a plea to ease his wife's labor pains realized that he had forgotten what he'd come for. He turned to the rebbe and whispered, "Rebbe! How does this story relate to me, I wonder?"

"It does! It does!" said the rebbe. "While you listened to the story intently, your wife delivered a healthy baby boy. Now go home and bring up your child steeped in our Jewish tradition."

Reb Motele Tchernobiler was amazed. "I am baffled," he said, "that you, Reb Yisroeltche, found it appropriate to tell this particular story."

"Why are you so amazed, Reb Motele?" the Rizhiner rebbe soothed. "The power of a story is mightier than the pen, and one can always walk away enriched from a good story."

Translated from the Yiddish by Miriam Hoffman. The material came from: 1) First volume of Tchernobyl: From the Rebbe's Courtyard, *published in Yiddish by the Jewish Book Publishing Company in New York by D.L. Meeker in 1931; 2)* Buon Appetito, Your Holiness: The Secrets of the Papal Table *by Mariangela Rinaldi and Mariangela Vicini. Published in 1998. Translated from the Italian by Adam Victor. Milano "Pope Joan" (circa 855–858) page 60–63.*

Zay nisht tsu zis vet men dikh nisht oyfesn. Zay nisht tsu biter, vet men dikh nisht oys-shpayen.

Don't be too sweet or you'll be eaten. Don't be too bitter or you'll be spit out.

The Moozhoyer Rebbe

by Miriam Hoffman

This true story took place in the sixties, in Brooklyn, on the twentieth anniversary of the liberation of the Ebensee concentration camp in Austria.

I found out about this solemn occasion by chance, spotting the announcement in the Jewish Daily newspaper *The Forward*. The get-together was conducted in the Moozhoyer rebbe's house in Brooklyn. I turned to my husband and said, "Mendl! Weren't you freed from the concentration camp in the town of Ebensee in Austria?" To which he replied, "Yes!"

"Then get yourself together," I insisted. "We're going." It took a lot of persuasion to get my Mendl to comply, until I said, "I'm going to record this occasion for my column in the *Yiddish Forward*."

Mendl agreed. So I took my little tape recorder and off we went. We found the Moozhoyer rebbe's modest, little house. It turned out that the rebbe used his enormous living room as a little synagogue. When we walked in, the room was already filled with men. The women must have been in adjacent quarters, but because I had to record this affair, I sat down right across the rebbe, among the men. Very soon, a young man came over to me and said in English, "Lady, you cannot sit here among the men! The women's section is in the back."

So I turned to him and, in my most innocent tone of voice, replied, "I am not a lady."

The young man got confused—who knows what he was thinking—and when he found his composure, he asked, "Then what are you?"

I said, "I'm the press," which confused him even more, so he left.

This time an older man confronted me in Yiddish: "Woman! You must not sit among the men; it is not customary."

So I answered him politely in Yiddish, "I am not a woman, I'm the press."

An assortment of young and older men confronted me with the same request and walked away confused and disoriented. I was kept sitting right across from the rebbe, whose bulging eyes were like spears piercing into me, but I didn't react. I just sat there among the men and embraced my newfound stature with great pleasure. Of course, my husband hid somewhere, not to be found.

The sermon began, and the rebbe waxed furious at the world that didn't protect us Jews from our greatest calamity. He also recited the *El Moley Rakhamim* (a prayer for the dead) and the afternoon was over. All the men dispersed, and the women remained behind the curtain busying themselves with household affairs. Suddenly, I heard the rebbe's loud voice calling in Yiddish, *"Presseh! Presseh!"*

When I realized he was referring to me, I turned around to face him. He gestured with his finger for me to come over his way, while he opened the door to a closet he had converted into an office.

I sat at a little table in his closet-turned-office. Of course, he kept the door wide open, in fear of being left alone with a female.

"Now," he said, "ask any questions you wish, and I will gladly comply."

So I turned to him and said, "I listened to your sermon about the annihilation of our people, so my question to you would be, where was God?"

Of course, this is the kind of question you don't put to a rebbe who has just finished sermonizing the greatness of God. He turned to me with a face of a winner and declared in a loud voice, "God had nothing to do with the Holocaust, and I'll tell you exactly who did."

I assumed he would intone "Hitler, the Nazis, our gentile neighbors who helped out in our destruction," but I was greatly mistaken. He turned to me triumphantly, pointing at me with the five fingers of his right hand and enumerating the following: "You know who brought upon us this disaster? The secular Jews, the communists, the socialists, the Zionists, the anarchists, the ones who rejected our God! Only they brought upon us this catastrophe, not God, blessed be His Name."

I sat there, almost turning into a pillar of salt, thinking to myself, *What is he saying? It's an abomination. It's a vile accusation!* My mind was muddled just for a minute. When I came to, I said to him, "I have one more question for you, Moozhoyer Rabbi, just one more and no more."

He looked at me as if to say, "Shoot!"

So I shot my question out with great anger, opening my fist and counting off the five fingers of my hand. "Now pray tell me, Rabbi"—I nearly choked on my words—"there were a million and a half innocent Jewish children murdered. They were not communists, socialists, Zionists, or anarchists. Why did they pay with their young lives?"

The rabbi straightened up, opened wide his glazed eyes, searching for an answer, then turned to me, and said, "We don't know God's ways of dealing with our world! So leave God out of it!"

On the way home, I asked my husband, "Where the hell is Moozhoy on the map? I never heard of a place like that!" Mendl calmed me down, saying, "OK. You know I was born in a *shtetl* called Bereksas (Berehovo), located between upper Apshe, Middle Apshe, Lower Apshe, and Apshitse in the Carpathian Mountains, between Hungary and Czechoslovakia, bordering on Romania. Ours was a small village, mostly populated by very pious Jews, who belonged to a Jewish sect called Vizhnitzer Hassidim.

"Now, close by, on the other side of the hill, there was a tiny little town called Moozhoy; I guess the population didn't exceed fifty families. So, this Moozhoyer rebbe, who puts on airs, pronounced himself the Moozhoyer rebbe, and it seems his Hassidim accepted him without any doubts.

"When the Germans came into our little town, they not only devastated the Jewish population, but it seems they cleared out every nook and cranny, wherever our people lived. So this man, who calls himself the Moozhoyer rebbe, wound up in the town of Ebenzee in Austria, where we all wound up after the death march from Auschwitz.

"I was a teenage boy," Mendl concluded, "and wound up among them when the American armed forces liberated us all, all of us skeletons, on the way out. So, I am thankful to this man who calls himself the Moozhoyer rebbe, no matter how he crowned himself. I regard him a fellow compatriot for remembering the day of our liberation."

THE WORST PRIDE
IS THE PRIDE OF
BEING PIOUS.

—REB MENDELE LUBAVITCHER

The Keys

In the city of Progeh, not far from Warsaw, in Poland, there lived a very wealthy man, learned in the Torah, a good and charitable Jew, called Fayvl Proger.

His wife, Rukhl Leye, was a righteous woman. She was a mother and a good earner, who kept busy with her little grocery store, thus enabling her husband Fayvl to sit day and night studying the holy books. Rukhl Leye did everything lovingly as long as her husband was able to sit and study Torah.

Then came a day when Fayvl passed away. The entire town was mourning, for Fayvl left behind a great name.

When Reb Fayvl reached heaven, it became clear to him that every Jew has an empty lot in the world-to-come and that each time he performs good deeds, those deeds are laid, brick by brick, onto that lot to build a heavenly home. The more good deeds, the more beautiful his heavenly abode turns out to be, until the house is done, surrounded by vineyards and orange groves—a real paradise. But if a Jew is not pious and doesn't observe the commandments and does no good deeds, what grows on his empty lot are stinging nettle and thorny brier.

But Reb Fayvl had a mansion with bright windows

and polished mirrors and mahogany furniture. The angel
Gabriel escorted him to paradise, leading him to his beautiful house.

When they reached the house, the door was locked,
so Reb Fayvl asked the angel, "Where are the keys to my
palace?" The good angel replied, "Reb Fayvl, my dear,
the keys remained down below in the lower world, in the
hands of your wife."

"With my wife, Rukhl Leye?!" exclaimed Fayvl. "What
are they doing there? After all, I did all the learning,
studying the Torah day and night doing all these good
deeds, so how come she keeps the keys to this beautiful
house in heaven?"

"You actually did all the good deeds," replied the angel
Gabriel, "but who worried about the livelihood? Who
brought up the children? Who gave you the money to do
charity?"

In short, Reb Fayvl had to wait at the threshold of
his fabulous house until his wife, Rukhl Leye, died and
brought with her the keys to their fabulous house in
heaven.

The Foolish Folks of Khelm

Khelm in Poland, although it still exists geograph-ically, is no longer a Jewish city. The Holocaust wiped Jewish Khelm off the map; almost all the Jews of Khelm perished in the Auschwitz and Majdanek death camps. But the memory of the Khelm Jews, both the wise and the foolish ones, will remain with us forever. So, although prewar Khelm was a real Jewish town in Poland, in our folklore setting, Khelm was known for its fools, the Khelemer naronim (the foolish folk of Khelm). They were the object of ridicule, yet always popular in their world.

But we didn't invent the town of fools. The Syrians regarded Homs as their Khelm of dullards; the Persians tell stories of Geelan as the town of simpletons; the Greeks had Boeotia, a city of incredibly witless folk; the French scoffed at their countrymen of Saint-Maixent-l'École; the Scots derided the men of Cupar in Fife; the Germans poked fun at the residents of Swabia and Schildberg; the Italians laughed at the inhabitants of Zago who fertilized the steeple of their church to make it grow taller; and even the good-natured Dutch ascribed stupidity to the Belgians.

Before we pass judgment on Khelm and other towns

of fools, listen to an alderman at a meeting at the city council of New York City in the 1940s:

"To beautify Central Park," he said, "I recommend we import gondolas from Venice, Italy, and let them swim around our lake in Central Park."

A second city councilman came up with a suggestion: "Take pity on the New York taxpayers! They are overburdened as it is, paying very high taxes."

A third councilman interrupted, "I would add an amendment to the suggestion. The idea of gondolas is perfectly brilliant, but it will cost too much. I suggest we import only *two* gondolas from Venice, a male and a female, and when they mate, we will have plenty of gondolas to go around."

P.S. Gondolas are small boats, in case you, like the councilman in this story, didn't know.

Zog nisht s'iz shlekht,
es ken alemol zayn erger.

Don't say it's bad;
it can always be worse.

The Khelemite Rebbe

One morning the Khelemite rebbetsn (the rebbe's wife) woke up from her sleep and didn't find her husband in bed, so she let go a great big scream, "*Oy Gevald* (help), the rebbe is missing! Where could he be? Woe is me!"

So the Khelemites set out to look for their rebbe, and suddenly they came upon a dead man without a head. So off they went to question the rebbetsn, wanting to know if the rebbe had a head. So the rebbetsn replied, "The rebbe used to smell his tobacco, and if one could smell, it's a sign he must have had a nose, but I am not too sure if he actually had a head."

So the Khelemites turned to the rebbe's beadle, his assistant, wanting to know whether the rebbe had a head, and he replied, "The rebbe used to pray under his tallis. Whether underneath his prayer shawl there was a head, I am not sure."

So the Khelemites set off for the bathhouse to ask the caretaker whether the rebbe had a head.

The caretaker thought for a while and answered, "To tell you the truth, the rebbe used to sit on the top bench so all I have seen are his feet. Whether there was also up there a head, I am not sure."

So the Khelemites paid a visit to the Khelemite Rov, their spiritual leader, well versed in the teaching of the Torah, inquiring whether the rebbe had a head. The rov demanded to know whether the rebbe had by any chance left a holy script behind and, if yes, that it be brought to him immediately. This way he would be convinced whether or not the rebbe had a head.

So the Khelemites searched and searched and finally came upon a *safer* (holy writ) that the rebbe left behind.

They brought it to the rov, who analyzed it from top to bottom and pronounced, "Khelemites, I can assure you, the rebbe had no head!"

The Flood

The story is told about the town of Khelm, where out of the blue, the heavens opened and unleashed a flood reminiscent of Noah's deluge. It nearly drowned everything in sight.

So the Khelemites took off to the rebbe's house with a plea. "Rebbe *Leybn* (long life to you, Rebbe), do something or we will all be wiped out, and not a sign will remain of us."

So the rebbe ordered them to say special prayers, imploring the One Above to stop this flood. But it became even more severe, as if God's wrath poured out of heaven, consuming the town of Khelm.

Finally, the rebbe came up with an idea. "Someone must be carrying on an illicit affair in the shtetl, so I command you to go and find the culprits who are committing this abominable sin! Only then will God's wrath be soothed."

So the Khelemites set out to find the culprits. They searched and ransacked every home, every corner of the town, until they came across a young yeshivah boy who had an illicit affair with a married woman.

In a fit of rage, they began cursing and throwing rocks at the sinful couple, intent on stoning them to death.

When the rebbe heard what they were doing, he came running, huffing and puffing, his fists in the air, shouting at the stone-throwing crowd, "*Gevalt Yidn* (God help us, Jews), what are you doing? You have as much brains in your head as the church has mezuzahs, you dunces! You idiots! You fools! You can't kill the couple! Think ahead, you dullards! What if next year we have a drought here in Khelm, and we need their services? What will we do then, you dummies? Ha!"

A JEW WHO IS A
TORAH SCHOLAR
CANNOT BE A HASSID.
AND AN IGNORANT
JEW CANNOT BE
A HERETIC.

—ANONYMOUS

The Khelemite Bridge

The witty, razor sharp political Zionist Dr. Shmaryahu Levin once said, "You want to know why we need a Jewish State? Then I will tell you a story: In the town of Khelm, the Jews wanted to build a bridge over the Khelemiter lake. So the Khelemer folk shouted, 'What do we need a bridge for?'

"The Khelemite merchants said, 'We need a bridge to do business with towns on the other side of the lake.'

"The Khelemite coachmen said, 'We need a bridge to carry passengers back and forth.'

"The Khelemite sons-in-law who didn't work but only studied in the synagogue and lived off the fathers-in-law's room and board said, 'We need a bridge to go walking and gawking at the moon on both sides of the lake.'"

In the end, Khelm remained without a bridge, and Dr. Levin finished, "Let us have a State. Later we'll figure out what we need a bridge for!"

The Khelemite Oven

On an ordinary old Wednesday, the Jews of Khelm decided to buy an oven for the synagogue. The problems were: where to put the oven, what the oven should be made of, and what would be the cost.

So between the afternoon and evening prayers (Tzvishn Minkha and Maariv – צווישן מנחה־מערב), they assembled to discuss the oven.

One of them said, "The oven should be made out of iron." Another said, "I insist it should be made out of tile."

But they had all decided that iron and tile were a bit too expensive when Berl, who came from the village, jumped up and said, "Gentlemen! I will help you. I am blessed with lots of animals on my farm. I have plenty of flour and butter, more than I need, more than I can sell, so I suggest you make your oven out of butter. I will donate it for free." The Khelemites were ecstatic, but one of them shouted out, "You must be crazy! The butter will melt in the fire!"

So the Khelemites reproached Berl. "You foolish Khelemites," cried Berl, "would you rather freeze to death?"

At this point, the rebbe of Khelm stood up and pointed a finger at everybody. "Gentlemen! Don't be so hasty. We cannot make an oven out of butter. It's impossible."

"But why, Rebbe, why?" everybody wanted to know. So the rebbe replied, "For the simple reason that come the Eve of Sabbath (Erev Shabbes – ערב שבת) when you are about to put into the oven a *tcholnt* (meat stew that cooks for twelve hours) and the oven is *milkhik* (dairy), you will have a *treyfenem* (non-kosher) oven on your hands. Have you thought of that?"

Beser tsu shtarbn shteyendik eyder tsu lebn oyf di kni.

Better to die standing than to live on your knees.

What Is a Skyscraper?

Three Khelemites attempted to explain to each other how tall the skyscrapers are in New York. Said one of them, "The New York skyscrapers are so tall that the snow remains on their roofs all year round."

Said the other, "That's nothing—a New York skyscraper has so many floors that people that live on the highest floor are required always to carry with them oxygen in order to be able to breathe."

Said the third, "What? You think that is amazing, you better listen. The New York skyscrapers are so tall that the Passover matzah must be baked on the holiday of Chanukah, because it takes from autumn until springtime to deliver them by elevator."

The Khelemer Melamed

by I. L. Peretz

Adapted and translated from the Yiddish
by Miriam Hoffman

There was once a time when the world was flooded with lust, pure unadulterated lust. Fear broke out among the Khelemites—"What if the Lord of the Universe will once again send down a flood, even though Noah and his ark was nowhere in sight?" So the Lamed Vov Tsadikim, the thirty-six righteous men in whose merit the world exists, decided to get together to discuss the sinful predicament they were in. They sat around for seven days and seven nights, thinking and deliberating until they came to a decision, namely to eliminate the *yeytser horeh* (evil inclination) altogether.

Let it be known that these Lamed Vov Tsadikim consisted of water-carriers, shoemakers, wood-choppers, chimney-sweeps, and stone-choppers—except for one among them, who had recently inherited a goodly sum from his aunt who had died in Alexandria in Egypt and who, having as yet had no time to let such a good fortune go to his head, decided to put the money to good use.

They came up with the idea of importing a 'Sris'—a eunuch from Egypt disguised as a good and pious Jew, complete with beard and sidelocks, prayer shawl and phylacteries, to engage in a teasing game with the Angel of Death, as if to say, "Go ahead and try to seduce me."

So the evil inclination spotted the Jew—beard and side-locks, what does he know?—and laughed out loud, "Kha! Kha! Kha! No big deal to tease and seduce one of them, beard and sidelocks . . ."

Having no idea that he was confronted with a eunuch, the evil inclination began his routine, first flattering the eunuch, then joking around with him, and then using profanities.

The eunuch was completely unaware of what was taking place. The evil inclination began to sweat and lose his voice, for this was the first time he had encountered such indifference. So he gave a whistle and conjured up a couple of floozies in hoop skirts, half naked, laughing and crying, but the eunuch remained unfazed. Frustrated, the evil inclination gave up and fell into a faint.

The moment the thirty-six righteous men spotted the predicament of the evil inclination, they grabbed him and tied him up with thirty-six *tsitsis* (tasseled undergarments worn by pious Jews). They slaughtered the evil inclination with a circumcision knife, threw him into a hot oven, and burned him to ashes. And when a stormy wind came out of the sky, the Jews took the ashes of the evil inclination and spread it all over the world.

Heaven rejoiced, earth was relieved, the nations of the world stopped declaring war, husbands and wives stopped bickering, the farming tools were used for baking Challah (Sabbath bread), cannons were made into scarecrows in the fields, and for the first time, the world tasted the joy of peace and tranquility.

Everything would have been hunky-dory, except for one thing: All men became gentlemen and all women virtuous ladies. The rabbis, cantors, and matchmakers went around without a stitch of work—no more wedding gowns, no more dowries, no more wedding feasts. All the men did was sit around in the synagogue studying Torah. People died, but no one was born.

If not for the Khelemer melamed, the teacher who taught little children the Torah, everything would have been lost; but that's not the end of the story.

Right before the gathering of the thirty-six righteous men, the Khelemer melamed suddenly felt the evil inclination driving him mad. It followed him everywhere— into the house of worship, the bathhouse, and wherever he turned. The evil inclination, may its name be erased, was always at his side, always accompanying him.

When the Khelemer melamed finally realized the evil inclination was winning, he decided to escape deep into the forest. He spent seven years of his life deeply entrenched in the wilderness, where he slept on the ground, ate roots, recited T'hilim (Book of Psalms), and threw himself into the study of Zohar (the mystical Book of Splendor). He lost a lot of weight and finally stopped seeing the evil inclination next to him. *It is high time,* he thought, *to return home.*

But the moment he came out of the forest, he

encountered a stormy whirlwind. This was precisely the time when the thirty-six righteous men spread the ashes of the evil inclination, and one tiny little speck flew into his left eye, which began seeing things he had never imagined he would see. It traveled from his left eye to his right eye, entering into his head and infiltrating the delicate strings of his heart. So the Khelemer melamed turned into the evil inclination, and once he returned to his shtetl, he infected the entire world with lust and passion.

My grandfather, peace onto him, used to say, "If not for the Khelemer melamed, the human race wouldn't have survived." And when my grandfather was invited to weddings and circumcisions, he used to say, "This is the work of the Khelemer melamed and in every one of us there is a spark of the Khelemer melamed."

So what's to be done? A young man in distress visited the rebbe, lamenting, "Oy vey, Rebbe, we live in a horrible world! It's disastrous, ruinous, and dreadful! What can be done, Rebbe?"

The rebbe listened intently, agreed with the young man, and came up with some advice. "You are right, my child. My advice is, go and change the world!"

Jauntily, the young man ran off to change the world. When he realized it was beyond his ability, he returned to the rebbe: "Oy vey, Rebbe, I cannot change the world! But when it comes to our shtetl, all I can tell you is that it's disastrous, ruinous, and dreadful! What to do?"

The rebbe listened patiently and replied, "Young man, my advice is that you go and change your shtetl."

A week went by, and the young man came back. "Oy vey, Rebbe, it's impossible to change our shtetl! It's so horrible, awful, and beyond repair. But when I think of it, even in my own household, no one gets along. We're always at each other, we don't trust each other—it's a hateful state of affairs. What to do?"

The rebbe smiled, knowing full well how difficult it was for a young man on his own to affect a change He thought it over and came up with this advice: "If that's the case, young man, then I would suggest you start changing yourself!"

Gey mol oys a toybn klezmer muzik,
a blindn di kolirn fun a regn-boygn
un a sris dem taam fun biye.

Go explain to a deaf man Klezmer
music, to a blind man a rainbow, and
to a eunuch the taste of an orgasm.

How Do We Straighten Out the World?

A shtetl *yidene* (a Jewish woman from a small town) was curious to know what her husband did day and night in the synagogue that had him always coming home late.

So one night she got a hold of him and went straight to the point. "Dearest! I want to know, what do you do day and night when you are not home? It seems you are always busy with meetings or *mikveh* (ritual bath), or the *hekdesh* (poorhouse), or the synagogue. Had I wasted so much time at all these get-togethers, I would have straightened out the whole world by now."

Her husband listened intently, considered her case and came up with a question, "What, for instance, could you have done that we men are incapable of doing?" Her answer came as swift as an arrow. "I would have fixed the world so that there would be no more poverty."

"And how, pray tell me, would you have accomplished this task, my wife?" the husband was curious to know.

"Very simply," she answered. "I would have married a rich boy to a poor girl, and the other way around, a rich girl with a poor boy. This way all the world's finances would once and for all be straightened out."

The husband thought his wife had hit upon a brilliant idea, so at the next community meeting, he proposed his wife's plan. Late that night, when the husband returned home, the wife couldn't wait to hear what he had to say. "So, how did it go?" she asked, full of excitement. The husband shook his head. "I'll tell you the truth, the poor folk were ready and eager, but we couldn't convince the rich guys. They were as stubborn as mules."

At Least One of You
Is a Mensch

coachman once came to a rebbe for advice. "What should I do with my horse, Rebbe?" he wanted to know. "The animal refuses to eat oats or hay! All he wants is *khalle* (Sabbath bread) and cake, *kreplech* (dumplings stuffed with meat), and *kneydlekh* (dumplings stuffed with cheese). What should I do with such an animal, Rebbe?" The rebbe observed the coachman and asked, "Tell me, good man, do you pray?"

"No, rebbe, how can I pray when I rise before sunrise? I'm too tired to pray."

"And when you are ready to eat, do you at least follow the custom of *neygl vaser* (the ritual handwashing upon arising in the morning)?"

"No, rebbe, my horse awaits me, my customers await, and my livelihood awaits."

"And do you say the *krishmeh* (the prayer said before going to bed)?"

"No, Rebbe, I come home late, tired and exhausted, and fall asleep."

So the rebbe pronounced his verdict: "Now I know why your animal wants sweets."

"Why, Rebbe?"

"It seems you behave like a horse! At least your animal behaves like a mensch.

A NON-BELIEVING JEW IS ALSO A JEW.

—ANONYMOUS

What Is a Bigger Trick?

The rebbe of Prague was once accosted by a madman who put a pistol to his head and said, "I want to see how the rebbe of Prague jumps out of the second-floor window and survives."

The rebbe of Prague listened to the demands of the madman and replied, "That is not a big trick! Everyone is capable of jumping from a second floor, but a greater trick, I would say, is to go down and jump up and reach the second floor."

The madman agreed, and the rebbe survived.

No One Dies of Hunger

In one of the *shtetlekh* (little towns), there lived a wise rebbe. One day, several people showed up and told him that Khaim-Yankl had died of hunger.

"What do you mean he died of hunger?!" the rebbe shouted. "After all he could have chopped wood, swept the streets, carried pails of water . . ."

He was told that the man had once been a merchant, so it was beneath his dignity to do menial work.

"If that's the case," the rebbe replied, losing his temper, "he didn't die of hunger, he died of pride! For if one is willing to work, one doesn't die of hunger."

The Town Preacher
and the Trustees

The city of Vilna (Vilnius) in Lithuania has no *rov* (traditional misnagdic, anti-Hassidic rabbinic sage). The Jewish community in Vilna does not hire a rov, which begs the question, "Why?" So the story is told thus:

Since Elijah, the Gaon (great sage) of Vilna (1720–1797), passed away, the trustees were not willing to bestow upon anyone else the honor of the title "Vilna Rov." On the other hand, how can a Jewish community, especially a Jewish city, remain without a rov?

There appeared once in Vilna a new town preacher, whose presence annoyed the town trustees to no end. They contended: "We ourselves have no livelihood to speak of, let alone an outsider! A preacher may take the bread out of our mouths."

The new preacher replied, "Don't fret! I will tell you a parable, so pay heed to what I have to say: Once a woman was in possession of a great big chicken coop. Days went by and she forgot to feed the chickens. On an ordinary Monday, the woman bought a rooster and threw him into the chicken coop.

"It so happened that a rooster is not a hen, and he demanded to be fed. He crowed 'CooCooReeCoo' and made a fuss and demanded his due. As soon as the woman heard the rooster crow without a stop, she remembered that she needed to feed the chickens. The same applies to me. As long as you were all alone in town, you were forgotten, but now, since I am here, I will crow, shout, and demand! I will preach until the city will suddenly wake up and acknowledge our presence, and from that moment on, we will live like God in Odessa, comfort and joy."

Gelt iz a vunderlekh artikl,
ze nor zolst nisht batsoln a
tsu groysn prize derfar.

Money is a wonderful thing:
see that you don't pay too
big a price for it.

The Man with Glass Legs

Reb Duvidl, the Tchernobiler rebbe, was a healer of the sick and a dispenser of blessings, amulets, ointments, and remedies, as well as being a mystic. All in all, he was a miracle worker.

One day, he was visited by a man who insisted he had glass legs and could not sit down for fear of breaking the glass, so he lived his life in an upright position. No matter how many times he was told he didn't have legs made out of glass, it was to no avail. People around him suspected that he was possessed by a dybbuk, an evil spirit, so he was taken to the Tchernobiler rebbe to extract the evil spirit from him.

The rebbe told him to sit down, and the man refused, wailing, "Rebbe, I cannot sit! My legs are made out of glass, and if I sit down they will crack."

So the rebbe shouted, "I order you to sit down! My command to you is sit down!"

The man shuddered and trembled with fear, but the rebbe had commanded him, so he sat down and instantly heard a crash of broken glass. The glass legs broke into splinters, and the man felt his legs were made out of flesh and bone as the Tchernobiler rebbe predicted.

"You see," said the rebbe, "the glass broke, but your legs remained intact."

The man was overjoyed and went home as if walking on air.

People were baffled and, turning to the rebbe, they asked, "But how did you accomplish this feat, rebbe?"

The rebbe replied, "While the man was about to sit down, I managed to notify my assistant in the kitchen to break a couple of dishes!"

It made the rebbe's disciples quite happy to know they had such a brilliant rebbe.

And That Was Enough

At times when a malicious decree appeared against the Jews, the holy rebbe Baal Shem Tov, Reb Yisroel of Mezeritch (1700–1760) founder of the Hassidic movement, would go deep into the forest and stop at a certain tree. He would light a small fire, and with great fervor, he would recite a prayer and a deeply felt melody to God, and that was enough; the decree would be abolished.

Years later, when the Baal Shem Tov was gone, once again there appeared a vicious decree against the Jews, so the Jews approached the magid (preacher) of Mezeritch and pleaded with him to intercede for their safety.

So the magid went to the same forest, and when he found the tree, he said a prayer with great melodic fervor and that was enough; the decree was abolished.

The next time a decree was issued against the Jews, the preacher of Mezeritch was already gone, so in his place, the rebbe Moshe Leib Erblich of Sassov went into the same forest and called out, "Dear God! We cannot find the tree any longer, and we cannot light that little fire any longer, and we cannot recall the sweet melody!" And that was enough.

Time passed, and once again a decree was issued against the Jews. At that point, the rebbe of Sassov was already gone, so Reb Israel of Rizhin took over. He stayed home, alone in his room, and said, "God Almighty, we do not remember any longer the forest, nor the tree, nor the kind of fire that was lit, nor the prayer that was said, nor the sweet melody that was sung. All we can do is retell the story and hope that will be enough."

When the Baal Shem Tov up in heaven heard this, he called out to God, "God of the Universe, how do I compare to him? How did I earn the right to sit next to such a blessed human being?"

*Dos lebn is an umheylbare
krenk vos foon ir iz nokh
keyner nisht aroys a lebediker.*

Life is an incurable disease
from which no one recovers.

A Story about
the Baal Shem Tov

The Baal Shem Tov, Reb Yisroel of Mezeritch (1700–1760) and the founder of the Hassidic movement, wanted to know who his neighbor would be in the world to come, so he pleaded with God to reveal to him this mystery.

When he found out his neighbor's identity, he took a horse and buggy and set off to find his neighbor, with a mind to get acquainted and have a chat with him concerning the Torah.

So he reached a small village, searched out his neighbor's meager abode, opened the door, and saw sitting at the table a healthy, strong, big-bodied man, without a beard or sidelocks, gorging himself on food and paying little attention to the guest at his door. He didn't even invite the Baal Shem Tov to sit down.

The Baal Shem Tov was greatly surprised, thinking, *How could this slovenly person be my neighbor in paradise?* He waited for quite a long time for the bloated man to stop eating. When he finally did, the Baal Shem Tov came closer to the man and asked him, "Please tell me, *Reb Yid* (mister), why are you eating so much?"

The man confided in him the following: "My father was a short, skinny little Jew. He hardly could catch his breath. When the gentiles came into our town, unleashing a pogrom on the Jews, they caught my father, tied him to a tree, and set him on fire. Within a split second, my father was scorched, that's how little my father was. And when I saw this, I promised myself I would not burn so easily. I will burn with a fire that will be seen from one side of the world to the other, Rebbe! That is the reason I eat so much."

And when the rebbe heard his tale, he called out to God, "Lord of the Universe, it would be my great privilege to have such a distinguished neighbor in Paradise!"

The Ladies' Tailor

It is said that Rabbi Eliyahu, the renowned *Vilner Gaon* (great sage of Vilna in Lithuania) (1720–1797) once called the ladies' tailor who lived on the same street, to his house, and said to him: "Moyshe, I would like you to chastise me!"

"Re, our crown jewel," said the tailor to him, "what are you saying—Moyshe, the tailor, should scold one of our greatest sages, the *Vilner Gaon*?"

"But I *do* want you to say to me that not everything I do is perfect. I'm not good enough."

So the tailor thought and thought, and this is what he came up with:

"Never mind. If the rebbe is willing, I will oblige, so listen to me, Reb Eliyahu. Then tell me, what is the big deal that you are a righteous man and a sage to boot? You sit in your room and you study and you pray—of course, it's easy for you to be a sage! But if you were a ladies' tailor like me, having to measure young ladies' and beautiful women's waists daily without having sinful thoughts on your mind, Rebbe, and still remain a sage—now that would be a greater accomplishment!"

DO NOT WEAR AN UPPER
GARMENT THAT CONSISTS
OF PRIDE, THE UNDER-
GARMENT OF RAGE IS
SEWN WITH STITCHES
OF DESPAIR.

—REBBE NAFTALI RAPSHITSER

The Rebbe
and the Israeli Bus Driver

Reb Yisroel was a pious man, a devout man, who followed all the commandments and led a very humble life. He taught young boys the Torah, and his *kheyder* (schoolroom) was always lively with young boys who couldn't sit still. They looked out the window and were envious of the children who were free to play ball.

But Reb Yisroel kept a grip on the boys and wouldn't let them out until late, after sunset, when the boys were exhausted and almost falling asleep—that's when he sent them home.

And so, one day Reb Yisroel died and went to heaven. He was told by the angel Gabriel, the keeper of the gates of paradise, to sit down and wait his turn. His neighbor in the waiting room was an Israeli driver whom the rabbi knew quite well. He knew that the man was not a devout Jew; he traveled and smoked on the Sabbath, ate non-kosher food, never visited a synagogue, didn't keep any commandments, and blasphemed God.

What is he doing at the gates of paradise, Reb Yisroel wondered, *sitting beside him waiting to be admitted first.*

But one doesn't ask any questions when it comes to heavenly justice; you just sit and wait.

Suddenly the gates of paradise were opened and the Israeli driver was admitted with great fanfare. The rebbe couldn't understand this injustice. He couldn't understand what was happening.

How come this godless, irreverent, sinful man is welcomed into paradise first, he thought to himself. I, the rebbe, was pious and devout all my life, ate kosher, kept most of the commandments, did good deeds, and lived with an ugly wife, and this mamzer (bastard) *was welcomed first into paradise? Where is justice?*

So the rebbe turned to the angel Gabriel with a heavy heart, and asked, "How come the Israeli bus driver has been welcomed to paradise, while I, Reb Yisroel, who kept most of commandments, ate kosher, did good deeds, and lived with an ugly wife all my life, am disregarded?"

The angel Gabriel took registered the rebbe's complaint and explained this puzzle to him: "You see, Reb Yisroel, you were teaching little boys the Torah and the commandments from morning till night, until the boys fell asleep, while this Israeli bus driver used to drive the bus with speed and swerve—you should have seen how his passengers prayed!"

Crazy Zeylig

In the small town of Shavel in prewar Poland lived Zeylig, whom everybody called "*Meshuggener* (Crazy) Zeylig." Whenever he was lucid, people used to ask him, "Zeylig, where does your insanity come from?"

So Zeylig would recall, "It might sound crazy to you, but I believe there is a God in heaven, and he sends down for each one of us a little bundle. One of us gets a full barrel of joy from his kids, and another gets a full bundle of heartache, and this is how the One Above distributes his goodies. As far as I am concerned, God sent me a bundle full of goodies. The only problem is that it all fell on my head."

Az ikh vel zayn vi er,
ver vet zayn vi ikh?

If I'm to be like him,
who will be like me?

Lilith, Adam's First Wife

God created Adam out of earth and dust, alongside Lilith, his first wife, whose name comes from the Hebrew word *Lilah*, meaning "night." Adam and Lilith were attached to each other by one spine, like conjoined twins. They stood up together and sat down together, but each possessed a separate brain. Lilith manipulated Adam with possessive, feminine thoughts, while Adam had masculine notions.

It was God who finally separated them, dividing them along their spine with a wave of his hand. After the separation, they felt like two separate individuals and could think for themselves.

One day, Lilith decided she was not going to lie beneath Adam while making love. Instead, she insisted on mounting him, which he took as an insult. Her independence annoyed him, and when he didn't comply, she flew away and settled along the Red Sea, bathing in the sun and having a good time on her own.

Adam flew into a rage—how dare she leave him?—so he complained to God, "What kind of a wife did you saddle me with? She has a mind of her own, and she left me, and now I am all alone! I am lonely and unhappy."

So God sent down three angels to look for her. It didn't take long; they found her sunning herself on the shores of the Red Sea, so they approached her, admonishing: "Lilith! How dare you leave Adam all alone? He is lonely and miserable. God is also very angry. You are commanded to go back to Adam."

Lilith listened attentively and laughed out loud. "No way will I go back to Adam! He is a bore, an empty vessel; he doesn't satisfy me! So be gone before I send Satan after you." So they were gone, and so was Lilith. She flew off into the heavenly constellations and thought of an innovative way to give birth on her own. She would come down to earth in the middle of the night and gather the wasted semen of young yeshivah boys as they masturbated, impregnating herself and giving birth to little demons.

As our mythology tells us, Lilith felt that she was wronged, vowing to take revenge on Adam's children by taking boys' lives on the eighth day and girls' lives on the twentieth day."

And so Jews were on guard when it came to birth mothers and placed above their heads amulets like the *Shir-Ha-maylesn*, the song of good deeds, verses from the Psalms and names of good angels, and also names of our patriarchs and matriarchs. All this was meant to chase away the demons.

Jews used to dress their little boys in girls' dresses and not cut their hair until they reached the age of three to confuse Lilith so she wouldn't know who was a boy and who was a girl. Women would be on guard against Lilith by guarding the birth mother for twenty-four hours after delivery. And before placing a young child into the crib for the first time, they put a black cat into the crib and then removed it to ward off Lilith. In the little towns and villages of Eastern Europe, young mothers would tie red ribbons and amulets around the wrists and necks of their newborn girls. On the walls of their beds would hang a blessing for the newborn. Today, observant, Jewish girls still wear red ribbons around their wrists.

And so, they all lived happily ever after,
Singing and dancing,
Drinking mead and wine
Believe it or not
It all went south
And never reached their mouth

‫- הָאט מען געהוליעט און געטאַנצט‬
‫- מעד און וויַין געטרונקען‬
‫גלייבט עס יאָ צי גלייבט עס נישט‬
‫איבער דער באָרד גערונען‬
‫און אין מויל נישט אָנגעקומען.‬

Lilith is also the name of a New York–based feminist maga-
zine because in its view Lilith was the very first feminist and
independent thinker.

A shverer baytl makht
a laykht gemit.

A heavy purse makes
for a light heart.

The Weeping Preacher

Just as there is a variety of cantors, there are also different preachers. There are preachers who are master orators, while there are others who speak and it sounds like a melody, while there are still others who excel in weeping.

As it happens, in one shtetl there was a preacher, a master throughout his career, who was so morbid that it was said the walls would shed tears while he himself used to weep, and the entire congregation used to cry together with him. Once, he delivered a sermon on how good it is to be good and pious and how bad it is to be bad, which caused the entire shtetl to go nearly mad.

To illustrate, he told them the following story: "Once there was a tailor, healthy and strong, as handsome as they come, who had a wife and seven children and worked very hard to eke out a livelihood. One day, his luck ran out. Even though he made a good living, he forgot what he was all about. He began to smoke on the Sabbath and eat non-kosher food until one day he pricked his finger with his needle while sewing. The blood began to flow until his right hand had to be amputated."

And as soon as the preacher finished, all the women began to cry. But the preacher did not pay any heed and kept spinning his tale:

"A week went by," he said, "and the tailor's left hand had to be amputated."

The entire synagogue was in tears, including the preacher, but he proceeded with his tale of woe. "And still the man didn't conform and didn't mend his ways. He lost all his money, his livelihood, until the town had to support him. A week went by, and his right foot had to be amputated."

The synagogue went into hysterics and the more the people cried, the longer the preacher preached.

"So you think the poor man changed?" he asked them. "Nothing doing! He went on until he lost his left foot and then one of his eyes and one of his ears, and he remained a cripple for life, but he never mended his ways! So, cry my friends, cry your hearts out as you hear the further misfortunes that befell this poor man. And if you think you've heard it all, you heard nothing yet."

The outcry of the people could be heard outside, and they kept on chanting, "What could be even worse than that?" And so the preacher went on, "Can you imagine, if that wasn't enough—a man without legs, without hands, without eyes and ears—what could have been worse than that? It was the time when the czar's army captured every available man to serve in the army; one day they came upon the poor tailor. They captured him, conscripted him into the czar's army, and made of him a soldier."

Now the entire synagogue was in tears. Everyone was weeping, flooding the synagogue with their tears, but can you imagine the greatest tragedy? The preacher couldn't swim, so he drowned.

The Grave of Reb Yisroel
the Deceased

ﬡ ot far from the Baal Shem Tov's grave in his home-
town of Medzhibozh stood an old tombstone on
which was inscribed, "Here lies Reb Yisroel the Deceased
who died during his life." There is a wonderful story
regarding this tombstone:

Hodl, the Baal Shem Tov's daughter, had four of her
own children: Reb Moyshe Chayim Efrayim Sudilkover,
Reb Burekhl Mezhibuzher, Reb Burekhl, and a daughter,
Feyge, who would become the mother of Reb Nakhman
Bratslaver.

After the death of Reb Yisroel Baal Shem Tov, it was
agreed on in Medzhibozh not to name a newborn baby
boy Yisroel; they believed that a boy given the name Yisroel would not live long.

But there came a day when Hodl's daughter, Feyge
(the Baal Shem Tov's granddaughter), gave birth to a
little boy. It is told that the Baal Shem Tov appeared in
Hodl's dream, pleading with her to name the newborn
Yisroel. On the other hand, Feyge refused to name her
newborn boy Yisroel, as she didn't want to endanger her
child's life. But Hodl wanted to fulfill her sacred father's

wishes, so when the cantor called out, "What will be the child's name in the House of Israel?" Hodl rose up and called out, "The child shall be named Yisroel!"

The cantor repeated her request and named him Yisroel against the mother's wishes.

On the third day after the circumcision, the child passed away. So Feyge, the unhappy mother brought the dead child to her mother, Hodl, put him down with tears in her eyes, and said, "Mother! You are guilty in my child's death, so here is the child. Do with him whatever you wish."

So Hodl took the child, brought him to the cemetery, put him down on her father's tombstone, and said, "Father, you were the one who instructed me to call the child Yisroel after you, and now he is dead. So take him, he is yours." She cried bitter tears and left.

It snowed all night long, and in the morning, when the gravedigger left his house, he heard the cry of a baby. So he followed the sound until he reached the gravesite of Reb Yisroel Baal Shem Tov and found the crying baby.

The town was in an uproar, and Feyge, the mother of the child, ran breathless to the cemetery and picked up her crying baby boy.

From then on, the boy was called Reb Yisroel the Deceased. He lived until he reached the age of one hundred, and when he died, he was buried in the same cemetery as his great-grandfather, the Baal Shem Tov, and on his tombstone it was written, "Here lies Reb Yisroel the Deceased who died during his life."

> ASSIMILATION! WHAT
> IS IT? IT IS COMPARED
> TO AN EXPRESS TRAIN;
> AT EVERY STATION, IT
> DEVOURS A BUNCH
> OF PEOPLE.
> —CHAIM NAHMAN BIALIK

Kiddush Hashem

Sanctification of God's Name

I t requires certain preparatory acts, one must come before the Creator purified, with all the symbols of Judaism intact. The Jews of the little West Galician town of Grodzhisk sincerely believed that pious and God-fearing Jews must arrive in heaven in one piece, beards and payyis (sidelocks) included.

In this little town of Grodzhisk, when the Germans ordered all the Jews to shave off their beards and sidelocks, the Jews cut off their beards and sidelocks and hid them in their pockets. They wished to come before the Creator as whole Jews. Little did they know that, before the Nazis shot them to death, they would be ordered to disrobe.

The Weeping Synagogue

by David Einhorn

Translated by Miriam Hoffman

ear a small Jewish town, hidden in a forest, stood an old wooden synagogue called the Weeping Synagogue. The synagogue was so old that no one prayed there any longer. The cobbles were overgrown with wild grass, and swallows built their nests on its bent roof.

It is told that at midnight, when all pious Jews rose for *Khtsoys*, to mourn and pray in the direction of the two temples in Jerusalem of old, they could hear a sound as if someone was quietly weeping in the abandoned synagogue. The elders used to say that a hundred years earlier, there once lived in this town a rabbi whose pious ways were known throughout the land. This rabbi was very poor, lived in a dilapidated little hovel not far from the synagogue, and sat in the synagogue studying the Torah day and night. Even when the entire village was asleep, the rabbi used to sit in the synagogue and study the holy scriptures by candlelight.

One midnight, sitting all alone in the synagogue, he suddenly heard a voice coming from the holy arc: "Your piousness and righteousness are being acknowledged in heaven. For your virtue, you are given one wish, which you must make at this very moment, so don't lose any time."

The rabbi was thrilled, thinking, *What should I wish? Wealth leads to greed, power leads to violence, honor leads to contempt. Should I wish for wisdom? The Torah is the greatest wisdom, and I am studying it day and night. No, I wish for naught.*

Suddenly he heard weeping coming from the holy arc, and the voice said, "You selfish man! All you had were selfish ideas and you did not think about mankind's suffering. You could have wished for the Messiah to come and redeem the world."

Next day, when the sexton opened the synagogue, he found the rabbi in a collapsed state. Once he was revived, the rabbi asked to see all the town's leaders. He told them what had occurred and then died on the spot. Thereafter, whenever the sexton opened the door of the synagogue, heavy drops would rain down from the ceiling and he would hear a low voice weeping, crying for the lost moment.

*A mentch zol lebn shoyn
nor foon naygerikayts vegn.*

Man should live if only
to satisfy his curiosity.

The Body and the Soul

Excerpts from S. An-sky's play The Dybbuk

One day there came to the town of Medzhibozh, where the Baal Shem Tov lived and died, a troop of acrobats, circus people, and contortionists who performed tricks with their bodies. They pulled a rope across the river, and one of them walked it without falling.

People were running to see the wonders of the performing acrobats, and along came the Baal Shem Tov to see the amazing feat. His students were amazed that the rebbe also had come to observe the great wonder of the day, so the Baal Shem Tov said to them, "I came to observe how a man walks across a deep abyss, and I thought to myself, *If only man would work as hard on his soul as he works on his body, how many deep crevices he could have overcome!*"

The Floor

This story happened in a small shtetl, population not more than five thousand. The town had a shul, a pretty nice synagogue, but with one impediment: the synagogue had no floor, an embarrassment before God and man.

So the young men of the town went to the old men and insisted that the synagogue needed a floor. All the old men said to the young, "You want a floor, make a floor! We have no money." But the young had no money either, so the synagogue remained without a floor.

One day, not a Sabbath and not a holiday, a preacher appeared in town, so the young ones went to see him and complained, "When you deliver your sermon, sir, please mention the fact that we have no floor."

The next day, the synagogue was full of people, and the preacher preached and preached until he came to the matter of the floor. "Keep in mind people," he said, "that the Messiah may come any day. He may come tomorrow, he may come today—today he will probably not come, but tomorrow he might come—and when he does come, there will be a resurrection, and the corpses will roll straight to our Holy Land and there they will all come to life. But the fifteen million of us living Jews, how will we get to Israel? I will tell you, dear friends, when the Messiah arrives, all the Jews will gather in the synagogues and we will all fly there.

"Wouldn't you want to know how we will fly? The angel Raphael and the angel Gabriel will make holes in the walls of the synagogue, and they will pull through the holes the wooden beams. So the angel Raphael will take the right beam on his shoulder, and the angel Gabriel will take the left beam on his shoulder, and they will lift the synagogue with all the Jews inside and fly us to our promised land. . . . But, if the synagogue is missing a floor, the synagogue will fly away, but all of you will remain outside."

Got helf mir aroyfkrikhn
oyfn layter
Arop vel ikh shoyn aleyn kenen.

God! Help me to go up
the ladder,
I can descend on my own!

The Prague Synagogue

The Prague synagogue was enormously big, and people tell many tales about it that are hardly believable. It is told that the synagogue was so big that when the beadle, the rabbi's assistant, wished to call up someone to the Torah, it was practically impossible for him to call the person from the Bimah, the stand from which the Torah is read, because the synagogue was so large that not all men were able to hear him. What to do? To solve the problem, the beadle decided to ride on a horse from one end of the synagogue to the other and call out the names of the men to come up and read passages from the Torah.

Another story regarding how enormous the Prague synagogue was went like this:

One day, someone came to Prague on the holiday of Hanukkah, and went straight to the synagogue. Believe it or not, they were still celebrating the holiday of Simkhas Toyreh and dancing Hakofes, the circular procession with the Torah scrolls in their arms.

Another told the story that the Prague synagogue had an enormous chandelier made out of amber, a gemstone that magically attracts straw.

There came a day when a wedding was performed in the synagogue, and the synagogue was filled with guests.

People began to search, and they soon discovered that the bride was hanging onto the chandelier. When they inquired, they discovered that she was wearing a straw hat, and the amber had pulled her upward together with her hat.

Vilnah Is a Big City

The city of Vilnah in Lithuania was known for its great Torah and secular scholars.

One day, a Jew ventured out to the city of Vilnah. When he returned to his shtetl, he didn't have adequate words to describe what he saw in the big city.

He was asked by the shtetl Jews, "So, tell us, what have you seen in Vilnah?"

"The Vilnah Jews are extraordinary people," he replied.

The small-town folk couldn't understand what he meant by extraordinary, so the man explained:

"I have seen a Jew who swayed back and forth over the Talmud, the sacred book of the traditional law, day and night. I have seen a Jew who pursued business day and night. I have seen a Jewish womanizer running after women day and night. I have seen a Jew run away from women as if from a wildfire day and night. I have seen a Jew who ran around day and night with a red flag, shouting, 'Revolution!' And I have seen a Jew who ran around shouting, 'Down with the Revolution!'"

So the shtetl Jews said to him, "Why are you so amazed? After all, Vilnah is a big city. Many Jews—all kinds of Jews—live in Vilnah."

The traveler replied victoriously, "What don't you people understand? I am talking about the same Jew!"

WHEN I DIE AND AM ASKED
IN THE WORLD TO COME
WHY I WASN'T MOSES,
I WILL REPLY, 'BECAUSE
I WAS TOO BUSY
BEING MYSELF.'

—RABBI ZUSYE TO HIS STUDENTS
(to help them see their potential)

The Mountain of Curses

This Mountain of Curses was located in the town of Nemirow, surrounded by a fence, smack in the middle of the marketplace, and here is what is said about it:

There was a rov, a rabbi, not a Hassidic rebbe, who was called by all the people Rabbi Yankev Yosef the Chastiser. He couldn't stand injustice and chastised everyone and was quick to punish, thus making many enemies.

So, on the eve of a Sabbath, his opponents caught him, sat him down on a garbage truck, and drove him far out of town. Not having any choice, the rov had to celebrate the Sabbath in the open field.

Next day, Sunday, he somehow made his way back to Nemirow, stood on a little mound in the middle of the marketplace, and began cursing, wishing on the merchants that their profits would disappear, and the marketplace would turn into a graveyard and be covered with wild grasses.

So the merchants stopped going to the marketplace, and as the news spread around, it became overgrown with wild grass, and from then on, it was known as the Mountain of Curses. The chastiser's maledictions had come true.

What About Those Little Crickets and Little Worms?

Take a good look, my child, how the One Above has set everything up," said the father to his child. "The birds lay their egg in their nests, and when they break out of their shells, out of the eggs come little birds. That's when the father bird and the mother bird begin to feed their young with little crickets and little worms, and they thank and praise the Lord for his exceptional goodness."

The child turned to the father and asked, "Father dear, do the little crickets and the little worms also thank and praise the Lord when the little birdies eat them up?"

Keyner veys nit vemen der shukh kvetsht, nor der vos geyt in im.

No one knows whose shoe pinches except the person who walks in it.

The Angel of Death

On the second day of Creation, God created the Angel of Death. This villain took on several names, among them Ashmeday (Asmodeus), Smal (Samael), Yeytser Horeh (evil inclination), the Malekh Hamash-khit (angel of corruption), and the Malekh Hakhoyshekh (angel of darkness). It is also said that perhaps Cain, who killed his brother, Abel, was transformed into the Angel of Death.

As a matter of fact, it is said that God not only created one Angel of Death, but six of them altogether. It is further said that among the angels, there are those who live forever and those who disappear. The angel Gabriel, for instance, is said to have banished some angels. The angel Kaptsie, it is told, shortened the lives of young boys, the angel Mashkhit shortened the lives of little children, the angel Mashbit took the lives of animals, and the angels Af and Khama took away the lives of people and cattle.

How did the ancients describe the king of the devils and evil spirits? They pictured him with empty eyes, a beard of serpents, and legs made of fire. He sports twelve wings, his span is from one end of the world to the other, Lilith is his consort, and they live on Mount Seyir.

Ashmeday, the Angel of Death, stems from Persia. His Name, in Persian myths is Ashmah Daedah: Ashmah is their god and Daedah is full of wrath and lies. In the Book of Tuviah, which was written in Greek, the devil is known as Asmodeus.

It is said in the Book of Ecclesiastes (Kohelet) that Ashmeday turned himself into King Solomon, banished the true King Solomon, and sat on the royal throne himself, pretending to be the king. As the story goes, King Solomon wandered through the streets of Jerusalem, dressed in rags and shouting, "I am King Solomon!" But no one paid any attention until they discovered that Ashmeday was sitting on the king's throne, whereupon they banished him and brought King Solomon back.

As is known, superstition has its own rationale, and we Jews have created a treasure trove of proverbs regarding the Angel of Death. Among them are these:

The Angel of Death slaughters and remains justified.

*In a house of a sick man, the Angel of Death
is free to roam.*

*When it thunders, it's a sign that demons are being
killed in Heaven.*

One of our curses says, "The Angel of Death should fall in love with him or her."

In Khelm, the town of fools, people didn't know where old age came from, so they speculated that it came from afar and decided to build a tower around the town.

When they saw that it didn't help, they decided to burn the calendar to prevent time from passing by, until they realized that old age was smuggled in by the Angel of Death.

It is said that the first gray hair is a notice from the Angel of Death, so with a tone of resignation we say, "Gray hairs are the flowers of graves."

It is also said that you can rely on the Angel of Death because he is punctual.

*A hunt shikt men nit
in yatke arayn.*

Don't send a dog to
the butcher shop.

Outwitting the Angel of Death

Based on Kurdistani Jewish Folklore

In a certain town, there lived a rebbe who spent day and night studying the Torah. He was the father of an only son. Once, in the middle of the night, he dreamed he saw the Angel of Death approaching his son, ready to snap up his soul. The rebbe awoke in a frightened sweat, but never dared to divulge his dream to anyone; it was his secret.

One day, an old man dressed in rags stopped in front of the rebbe's fence and declared, "I am the Angel of Death! I was assigned to take your son's soul, as he has come to the end of his days."

The rebbe shuddered and wondered how he might break this ugly decree when suddenly it occurred to him. He turned to the Angel of Death and divulged a little secret: "Know that my son is about to celebrate a great occasion. He is about to get married, so I beg of you not to interrupt the joy of our celebration!"

"Very well!" the Angel of Death conceded. "I will do my task after the wedding." And he disappeared.

So the rebbe busied himself preparing the greatest of feasts, with wines, and liquors, but he did it all with a heavy heart. Then he came across an elderly man who said to him, "I know that your son's life is in danger;

101

therefore, I urge you to soften the heart of the Angel of Death. Offer him wine and whiskey, get him drunk, and feed him the best of your refreshments and delicacies!"

Once the Angel of Death was happily satiated, he approached the groom and said, "Many years ago, I borrowed some people's straw. I mixed it with clay, and I used this concoction to build me a house. Today I was approached by the man, and he demands I return the straw to him. What should I do?"

So the bridegroom answered, "Buy other straw and return the straw to the owner."

"Yes!" the Angel of Death exclaimed. "But the guy insists he wants the old straw back, not the new straw."

"I advise you," said the groom, "to destroy the house and return the old straw as he demanded."

"The straw," said the Angel of Death, "happens to be your soul and God wants it back."

"If this is the case," answered the groom, "give me some time. I must say goodbye to my folks, especially to my new bride." When the family heard this awful news, they began pleading with God. But the bride approached the Angel of Death and said, "According to the Torah, it is written that a bridegroom is forbidden to go into battle and lose his life an entire year after his marriage vows."

As soon as the Angel of Death heard this, he took off in a hurry to hear God's verdict. Suddenly he saw two angels standing in front of God's throne, pleading with Him to save the young groom. God's heart melted when he realized that the groom was wise and pious, so he sent the Angel of Death on another errand.

The Son of
the Angel of Death

There was a time when the Angel of Death came down to earth and married a Jewish woman, a real witch of a wife. They lived together for many years until she bore him a son. When the son turned fifteen, his father, the Angel of Death, got bored with his wife, the shrew, and found he preferred Hell instead of her.

But he loved his son, so he turned to him and said, "I advise you to become a doctor. When you visit a sick patient who will not survive, you will see me standing at his head as a sign he will not make it. If you do not see me, it will be a sign that the patient will make it." That said, the Angel of Death disappeared.

The son did become a doctor, well known the world over. As time went by, the king of the land became ill and no doctor could help him, so the son of the Angel of Death was called and was told, "If the king of the land does not make it, you will pay with your head."

The son agreed and proceeded to examine the king. His pulse was slow and his breath even slower. Suddenly he spotted his father, the Angel of Death, at the head of the ill king. He shuddered and said to him, "Father! Get out!"

"The king must die!" his father replied.

When the son realized his father was not moving, he reproached him, "Father! If you don't get out of my way, I will be forced to call Mother."

As soon as his father heard his son's warning, he disappeared. The king got well, and the son became rich.

*Di eyer viln zayn kliger
fun di hiner.*

The eggs think they're
smarter than the chickens.

*Der mentsh trakht
un got lakht.*

Man plans and
God laughs.

Poking Fun

ow did the pious Jews poke fun at the newly sprung intellectual, secular Jews? Instead of intelligentsia, they were called shmentelligencia. Instead of educated, they were called shmejucated. They also called them shmadkep, converts, little Germans, non-koshernikes, and devourers of milk products with nails. Why nails? Because nails were sharp, as if to spite the One Above. They would call a secular unmarried woman of a certain age "a newish Jewish old maid."

How did the secular Jews poke fun at the pious Jews? Instead of *"Reboyne shel Oylem,"* meaning "Lord of the Universe," they called them *"Reb Yoyne shel oylem,"* meaning "Rabbi Yoyne of his own little world." Instead of *"Olev hasholem,"* meaning "peace be with the deceased," they said, *"Olev Hashnoble,"* meaning "the beak (long nose) be with him." Instead of *"Loshn Koydesh,"* the sacred tongue, they said *"Lokshn Koydesh"*—sacred noodles. Instead of *"She-eyn-ish"*—where there is no man—they said *"Iz hering oykh a fish,"* meaning "a herring is also a fish."

Verter zol men vegn
un nit tseyln.

Words should be
weighed, not counted.

About the Author

Miriam Hoffman earned her first baccalaureate (B.A.) in 1957 from the Jewish Teachers Seminary in New York, which was accepted at the New School for Social Research in New York in 1981, upon her return from a decade living in Israel. In 1982, she earned her second B.A. at the University of Miami.

In 1982, Miriam was accepted at Columbia University of New York and majored in Yiddish folklore and literature, where she did all her graduate work. Today she is Professor of Yiddish language, literature, Jewish culture, Yiddish humor, classical and minor Yiddish writers, and a course called 20th Century Yiddish Literature and Film. She taught at Columbia University from 1992 to 2015.

Miriam is the author of *A Breed Apart: Reflections of a Young Refugee,* the highly personal and historic account of the author's life that brings to light the oppression of the Soviet regime, the five-year history of the Displaced Persons Refugee Camps (DP camps) in Germany from 1946 to 1951, the struggles of post–World War II anti-Semitism, and her coming of age in America.

She has also written a Yiddish textbook called *Key to Yiddish,* which includes scholarly research, conversation, folklore, folktales, songs, and literary works by the most acclaimed Yiddish writers and poets. *Key to Yiddish* also contains humorous illustrations that appeared in the Yiddish magazine *Der Groyser Kundas,* in print from 1911 to 1929.

The Author Graduating Workmen's Circle Mitlshul (2nd row, 1st from left)

The very last chapter in *Key to Yiddish* includes Miriam's successful play called *The Maiden of Ludmir,* which deals with the first female Orthodox rabbi in the Ukraine of 1805–1892. *The Maiden of Ludmir* was performed at the Folksbiene Theater. *Key to Yiddish* is now used in many universities all over the world.

Miriam is also a successful Yiddish playwright. She has written many plays including *Reflections of a Lost Poet,* which deals with the life and works of the most beloved Yiddish poet Itzik Manger and which is still being performed today both in the United States and Israel and, as of 2016, is being staged in Bucharest, Romania.

Miriam has written several plays with Rena Borow, among them the play *Noble Laureate.* Isaac Bashevis-Singer was the Nobel Laureate for Literature in 1978, and the play is named after a since-corrected misspelling on his tombstone. The play tells of Isaac Bashevis-Singer's battle with dementia in the declining years of his life in Miami Beach, Florida. It was performed at the Queens Theater in the Park in New York City.

Miriam's plays were also staged at the Folksbiene National Yiddish Theater of New York, The Yiddish Theatre of Saidye Bronfman, the Centre for the Arts in Montreal, Canada, and the Yiddishpiel Theater in Israel. Miriam is the recipient of the Israeli Tony Award for her Yiddish translation of Neil Simon's *The Sunshine Boys.* Her Yiddish translation of Mel Brooks's *The Producers* was performed to great acclaim in 2016. It ran for several months to sold-out houses at the Dora Wasserman Yiddish Theater and the Alvin Siegel Center in Montreal, Canada.

Miriam is also a known Yiddish journalist and worked as a feature writer for the *Yiddish Forward* from 1982 to today.

The years 2014–2015 saw Miriam's retirement from Columbia University after twenty-five years of dedicated work. Since then, she is still busy writing her column for the *Yiddish Forward*, and working on a new Yiddish play called *Shiklgruber and Dzugashvili*, the original names of Hitler and Stalin, a musical comedy in two acts. Miriam still lectures on the topic of "Yiddish in Living Color."

OTHER BOOKS BY PROFESSOR MIRIAM HOFFMAN

Key to Yiddish

Key to Yiddish aims to introduce the student to the fundamentals of Yiddish language and culture.

It contains idiomatic constructions, dialogue, selected readings, exercises and worksheets, all geared to welcome the student to the world of Yiddish, its history, tradition, customs, rituals, songs, and holiday celebrations.

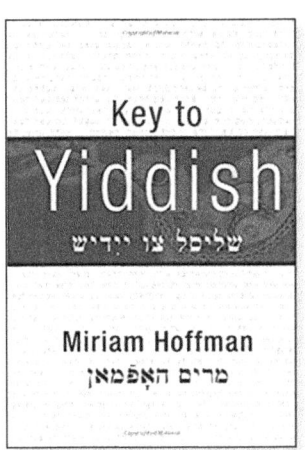

A Breed Apart: Reflections of a Young Refugee

From Siberia to Columbia University, this epic tale of war and survival is seen through the eyes of a young Miriam Hoffman and her father, Chaim Schmulewitz, a well-respected columnist of the Yiddish press *Undzerweg*.

Highly personal and historic, *A Breed Apart* brings to light the oppression of the Soviet regime, the Displaced Persons Refugee Camps (DP camps) in Germany from 1946–51, the struggles of post–World War II anti-Semitism, and the author's coming of age in America.

Legends of the AlefBet

Legends of the AlefBet: The Origins of the Alphabet is Professor Miriam Hoffman's epic examination of the origins of written language.

At Columbia University, Professor Hoffman spent decades researching the folklore and legends of the ancient Hebrew and Yiddish alphabets. Now, utilizing and illustrating that research, Professor Hoffman entertains and educates her readers with the amazing stories that illuminate our modern languages.

Utilizing the original 1919 artistic serigraphs of master artist Ben-Tsiyon Zuckerman, as well as the colorful Alefbet of master artist Michoel Muchnik—plus additional artistic and related imagery—each letter is examined through its history and the literary and artistic depictions that surround it.

This masterfully enlightening historical and academic work provides readers with scholarly insight into our modern languages and cultures.

ALL AVAILABLE ON AMAZON.COM